SEXUALLY EXPLICIT STORIES:

BDSM, CUCKOLD, DIRTY AND MORE FOR ADULTS

Vol.5

by Rebecca Sin

I would like to invite you to read another one of my books that I think you will really enjoy. The book is called:

"FILTHY SEXY STORIES FOR ADULTS:
10 Short Exciting and Spicy Stories"

Enjoy!

Table of Contents

BEAUTIFUL CARRIER

The Carrier and Divorced Man

About five years ago, my wife and I decided to get a divorce. We married young, and were also married to our careers. We had no children, because neither one of us would be home long enough to be a good parent. Our sex life was pretty good, when we happened to be together to have sex. We divorced the best of friends.

I thought it would be a good idea to do a Bob Seger and "Turn the Page." Since I had relatives on both coasts, a move to the Midwest was my choice. No more long coast-coast trips. I bought a house an hour's drive south of a major city. As long as I owned a dependable car, and could get to an airport, I could work from just about anywhere in the country.

One day, a couple of weeks after I moved in, the doorbell rang. Standing at the front door was a very pretty Postal Worker carrying a package. She said, "Hi, my name is Marty. Whenever possible, we have to hand deliver packages." I thanked her, caught a hint of Lavender, and watched her slim figure, complete with bouncing ponytail, get in her vehicle and drive to my neighbor's mailbox. We were close in age, but I thought I was about 5 years older.

Over the next month, Marty delivered a couple of

packages, and found the time to make small talk with me. One afternoon, I was working from home, sitting on my patio reading a spread sheet, and drinking a glass of wine, when my doorbell rang.

Marty was standing on my front porch with a package. When I opened the door, she said, "Tony, I tried to deliver this yesterday, but you weren't home, I was afraid it might get wet, so I didn't leave it." I responded, "That's fine and if I'm not around, which happens frequently, that's what you should do. She then said, "I notice all the mail is addressed to you, are there a Mrs.?" I told her that I was divorced and unattached, but married to my job.

Hearing this she quickly said, " My girl friends and I go to the Midway Cafe on Wednesday nights. The beer is cold, sometimes there's live music, and there are significantly less guys trolling the place looking for a piece of ass!" I already liked her bubbly personality, now I was enjoying her candor.

"You know," I said, "I just may see you there."

The following Wednesday around 9:00, I walked into the Midway Cafe. Almost every animal that once lived in the county was stuffed and on display. The only thing missing was Patrick Swayze! When Marty saw me, she shrieked and came running up to me. She gave me a big hug, a sisterly kiss on the cheek, and took me by the hand to her table.

Introductions were made, rounds of beer were purchased, and everyone seemed to be enjoying themselves. Marty's crew were all single; one friend never got married, one friend was divorced, and one friend was a military widow. Marty got up couple of times and unsteadily walked to go to the bathroom. When she came back the last time, she asked me, with slurred words, to take her home.

I parked at her apartment complex and walked her to her door. I could smell the clean fresh Lavender shampoo she used on her hair. She looked at me and said, "Would you like to come in?" As much as I wanted to, I said, "Marty, if we're going to bring our friendship to the next level, we are going to do this right. I'm a bit of a Foodie and I know my way around a kitchen. You will be wined and dined by candle light. I've never taken advantage of a girl in my life - I'm not going to start with you."

She hugged and thanked me for being a gentleman. I watched her, in her tight jeans, enter the apartment. I waited until I heard the door close and the lock set, then I went home and seriously thought about jerking off.

It was almost three weeks before my schedule would allow us to have that supper I promised.

Marty showed up wearing a t-shirt, skinny jeans, heels and her signature pony tail. "My goodness", she said, "This house smells like an Italian Restaurant!"

I poured us a glass of wine that paired well with the supper I prepared, and showed her around the house.

We sat in the living room sipped our wine and made small talk; mostly about how much she liked the completely open kitchen, dining room and living room concept of my house.

I asked her to light the candles and refill our wine glasses, while I opened another bottle of wine and plated supper.

During supper, she told me about her ex. I told her about my ex. She talked about work. I talked about work. She mentioned not dating much since her divorce. I mentioned not dating much since my divorce. She told me about growing up on a big working farm. I told her about growing up in a big east coast city. She told me that if she ate anymore, she would explode. I told her to save room for dessert!

I said to her, "Let me clear the table, then we can have cordials in the living room. When we have digested properly, we'll have the dessert I made. I can turn on the fireplace for ambience."

We each took something to the sink, multiple times. I finished loading the dishwasher, and turned to find Marty standing very close to me. She undid her ponytail, shook out her hair, and wrapped her arms around my neck.

Our first kiss was passionate and tender. Her lips were soft and moist. Neither one of us was in a rush to do anything more, but kiss. Eventually our tongues began exploring each other's mouths. Our breathing began to quicken, and all the while, I could smell the unmistakable Lavender scent of her hair.

"The rest of the clean-up can wait," she said. "Let's go

mess up that nicely made kingsize bed you have in the master bedroom."

I led her by the hand to the foot of the bed and we began kissing again. This time, our hands began to explore the contours of each other's bodies. I hadn't been with a woman in some time and my dick was straining to be released from my pants.

Our tops came off first; her's, followed by mine. Marty began kissing my chest and licking my nipples. She reached behind her back and unsnapped the claps on her navy bra. Her perfect B cup tits with their big pink nipples were inches from me. Our chests came together as we continued our slow, tender kissing.

I sat on the bed and took off my shoes and socks. I stood to remove my pants, then sat back down. My underwear did little to conceal my hard dick. Marty stood in front of me, stepped out of her heels and wiggled out of her jeans and navy panties. Standing before me was an incredibly beautiful and sensuous woman. Her nipples were hard, and her thighs framed a swollen pussy, with a dark brown landing strip.

She reached for my underwear and when I raised my ass, she took them off. My dick sprang straight up. She knelt next to me on the bed, and we started kissing again. She slowly rubbed my balls before grabbing my dick. My pre-cum acted as a lube, as she began stroking me. Sensing that I would unload soon, she gently pushed me on my back and covered my face with her pussy. Before she took me in her mouth she said,

"Please don't come in my mouth, but anywhere else is fair game."

I ran my tongue along the edges of her pussy. I licked up and down her wet gash. My senses were in overdrive. Even here was a hint of Lavender. My dick was the hardest its even been. She was as deliberate, gentle and slow, sucking my dick as she was when kissing me. I felt her lips on the base of my dick, as she took me deep in her mouth. With each stroke, I got closer to exploding. With each stroke, I pushed my tongue into her wet pussy.

I told her when I was ready to cum, she removed my dick from her mouth and stroked me fast and hard. I continued to lick her as I deposited a load of cum on her chest and my lower body. I felt her legs quiver and her ass begin to bounce. I realized she was having her own orgasm. I ran my tongue up to her ass-hole. I continued licking her there until she came again.

She collapsed on top of me and said, "Dear God, That's the most sperm I've ever seen at one time. How long have you been storing that up?" "I really can't remember the last time I came," was my response.

We were both covered in cum and decide to take a shower together. I have an oversized shower. The previous owner made the bathroom handicap assessable. We soaped each other up, cleaned each other off and stayed under the shower head holding each other and kissing, until the water started to get cold.
After drying off, we headed back to the kitchen, naked. Once the kitchen was clean and the dish washer running, we took our cordials to the living room. I sat and Marty laid down facing the fireplace, with her head on my thigh.

Sitting there, watching the flames dance, I began rubbing her shoulders, her side, and her pretty ass. I started to get hard, again. The gentle touching was having an effect on both of us. When Marty saw my full erection, she positioned her mouth over the head of my dick, and began licking me. When she stopped, she said, "I want to feel you inside of me."

Right there on the couch, we fit together like two puzzle pieces. I entered her and began slowly pushing my dick all the way in and almost completely out. Marty met each of my strokes with one of her own. Her orgasm was strong, and loud. "I've never had so many orgasms, in one night," she said.

We left the couch for the bedroom. We continued our love making, and as corny as this sounds, we didn't fuck like two rabbits, we made passionate love to each other. I held her arms above her head, licking her nipples as I continued to slide in and out of her. When I stiffen, she contracted her pussy and I deposited my load deep inside of her. For the longest time, we stayed in that position holding each other tightly.

Marty eventually went into the bathroom, cleaned herself up, and returned with a warm wash cloth. She cleaned her juices and any left over cum off of my dick, and said, "Tonight was wonderful, can I stay?"
I said, "Of course."

We woke up in the same position we fell asleep in; me wrapped around her with my dick resting against the cheeks of her perfectly shaped ass.

Six months after this glorious evening, our time together ended.

One afternoon, my door bell rang. Marty, my Lavender Lady, was standing at my door without a package and tears in her eyes.

"Marty come in, what's the matter," I asked. In between sobs, she said, "My Mother suddenly passed away. I'm her only child and inherited the family homestead. I'm going home. It's a permanent move. I've already submitted my transfer papers, in case the farm is too much for me to handle and I have to sell." We held each other tightly. I tried to summon the right words to say, but I was having a difficult time processing what I just heard. This in all likelihood was our good-bye.

I threw caution to the wind, and while inhaling deeply her Lavender scent, I said, "You are the most amazing person, I've ever known. Your personality and laugh are infectious. I fell deeply in love with you and I will never forget you or our brief time together."

Tears ran down her pretty face and she said, "I never met a man like you. You are the best thing that's ever happened to me. I love, and will never forget you."

We held each other tightly and kissed one last time. If she wanted to stay that night, she could have. Asking her to stay, one final time, would just prolong the inevitable.

She slowly opened the door, turned to face me, and said, "My friends and I have no secrets. They know all about us. Don't be surprised when those heifers start showing up at your door!"

Thankfully, my job kept me busy traveling. There were stretches of time when I was away from my home, more than I was home. About 4 months after Marty moved, I bumped into Rita, one of her friends who said, "We don't hear from Marty anymore. She told us that making a clean break was what she needed to do. It was time to "Turn the Page," or some such thing."

Rita, also said, "We still meet at the Midway Cafe on Wednesday nights. The beer is cold, sometimes there's live music, and there are significantly less guys trolling the place looking for a piece of ass! We have an extra seat at our table, if you're interested."

CARING TEACHER
Teacher and Student

I walked into English literature as usual and sat down at my desk, it was thankfully right at the back of the classroom so I didn't have to bother with the lessons as much. I so couldn't be bothered with this lesson, our teacher had been off ill for ages and we hadn't even completed the revision for our exam that was in three weeks. I took out my anthology as the other students filed in, they all looked as sick to death as I was. I began reading some poems before the class fell into its usual drowsy state, it was the end of the day and as it was winter it was getting dark early, and the Head teacher put the heating up so high you felt yourself nodding off.

My best friend, Katherine, sat two desks in front of me and threw a note at me which hit me square in the forehead making her laugh. I unfolded the crumpled piece of paper frowning at her, secretly very glad no one saw the paper hit me as I would have went red. It had scribbled across it in her writing this:

"Lottie!! The sexiest man alive will be coming into the classroom in at least 3 minutes time. Love K x"

I looked up at her and she winked then tapped her wrist watch. I looked around and none of the other girls seemed to be awaiting a gorgeous guy, so what the hell was Katherine going on about. I opened my desk and pulled out my note pad and gel pens, I thought why not doodle seeing as I have nothing else to do. I uncapped a gold glittery pen and began to drawing on my notepad and I looked up as the classroom door opened.

Two men stood in the doorway, shit head Mr.Grandthorpe and a someone who had their back to the class, this must be him. He had a nice bum, and broad strong shoulders and muscular arms. I strained a little to get a better look but failed as everyone in front of me seemed to be doing the exact same thing, I sat back in my seat, disappointed.

They were muttering about something so I slid my things back into my desk and looked at Katherine who turned around and fanned herself with her anthology, fluttering her eyelashes playfully before turning back around to stare at the man. I wish I could see his face, go away Grandthorpe you loser! Then he looked up, no not handsome backed man, but Grandthorpe, straight at me.

"Why do you not have your anthology out?" he drawled, his voice was like oil, or gloopy ink running towards me at a sloth pace through the room, all of his words dragged out. I glared at him and felt my cheeks blush slightly as the other man turned around, he was breathtakingly gorgeous. Grandthorpe entered from the doorway, his B.O filling the room making me want to wretch.

"Well seeing as we in fact haven't had a teacher for about...6 months then I'd like to announce I've learned it all by heart." Both men just stared at me and then the gorgeous man spoke.

"Well, it's a good thing that I am taking over, hopefully you'll have the same amount of dedication to the Lord of the Flies book which you'll be studying with me, we've delayed the mock exam you are having also so to give you all time to catch up as well, I do hope your pleased Miss -"

"She's called Charlotte. She has a wicked mouth on her so you're best to keep your eye on her."

"I think he meant your ears Sir, as using your eyes to listen to my wicked mouth wouldn't be very clever, would it Mr. Grandthorpe? Also, I prefer being called Lottie." He glared at me and the apparent student teacher grinned, his green eyes staring at me twinkling.

"See what I mean? Lottie indeed! I best leave you to introduce yourself, school finishes at 3.10 pm. Goodbye class." Mr.Grandthorpe glared at me and left at the students mumbled goodbyes. I then returned   my attention to the gorgeous student teacher.

He walked to his desk, all of the girls giving him an amazing amount of attention as he did this, and put his files in his desk drawer.

I couldn't take my eyes off him, he had a manly chiselled jaw with stubble which made him look even better, and his hair was slightly messy, as though he had just gotten out of bed, this made me think of... well lets not think about that, he's a teacher I reminded myself. His eyes were a gorgeous green colour, I was mesmerised by him to be honest. I was just staring at him, my mouth slightly open, he must have noticed every female looking at him.

"Well class, I'm Mr...never mind that, I'm Steven,I prefer Steven to be honest. Today we're going to get to know each other instead of studying the boring stuff. So, um, lets start with you."

He pointed at a flustered Katherine who began to giggle strangely. I snorted at this and so did the rest of the class, the gibbering fool.

"Your name?"

"Oh, Katherine Smith."

"Lovely too meet you." he smiled at her and his flash of white teeth stopped every girl in the room. I wasn't able to tear my eyes away from him.

"And you?" he was going round the entire room, making all the girls turn to mush and all the boys try to turn on some macho persona to compete with him. Then it came to me, my turn to introduce myself, although I didn't need to.

"Lottie, hello again."

"Hello." I said smiling, trying to prevent my cheeks from turning into two red apples.

"Now, it would seem I already know your name...hmmm, tell me something else about you?"

I looked at him and all that went through my head was you're gorgeous and I can't believe I even have your attention! This amazingly sexy man was looking at me with a slightly raised eyebrow, the corners of his smooth lips curling into a cheeky smile, slight dimples appearing in his cheeks making me melt.

"Well Lottie? I am your teacher and I demand you to take part in this exercise just like everyone else." Our eyes never tore away from each other, we were staring and the class noticed too.

Katherine spoke up.

"Lottie fancies someone in the class, there's a fact for you Steven." she cooed, grinning at me and winking. I went red. Some of the girls giggled and Steven raised his hand to silence everyone.

"Now, who is the boy? Or girl?" he said, a playful tone in his voice that only I seemed to have caught.

I opened my mouth to argue that I was not gay but Katherine spoke up again

"Oh its someone who's a little bit out of reach for her-"

"Shut up." I said, Katherine couldn't possibly know that I fancied him, he'd only been in the room fifteen minutes.

"Come on then Kathy, who do you think I fancy then?" I dared her, and she smiled and shrugged. I crossed my legs and pulled my pleated skirt into place, I noticed his green eyes trailing slowly up my bare legs and then catching my eye.

"I don't know Lottie... you never said his name."

I felt relieved that she wasn't going to embarrass me further. Stevens's gaze was still on me and I could feel sweat gathering on my skin. Why was he so good looking? Why did he keep staring?
"Oh well then, we'll keep that for another time." He winked and I gasped, why did he wink? Did he know I fancied him? I was suddenly thinking rude thoughts about him. What did his body look like under that shirt? And how I liked the way his brown eyes

glimmered when they became amused or interested... and how he couldn't take them away from my legs or chest.

He's a teacher I reminded myself. But I wanted him all of sudden, not just finding someone attractive... but lusting after him.

I gulped as I watched him write on the board, his muscles flexing. He told the overly eager girls at the front to hand out the books, they all swooned but he didn't take any notice. We were a class of 18 year old girls acting like love sick 14 year olds every time he moved, or flexed a bicep. I even became jealous when he gave another girl student any attention, but he always made glances towards me.

We read the first chapter of the book, but I couldn't concentrate as he paced the classroom, brushing his hand on my shoulder as he passed, and even stopping to ask how I was doing, his breath on my neck making me shudder, the way I noticed him licking his lips as I read. I glanced at him, why was he doing that? Why was he making me focus on his lips?

Then the bell rang.

It was the end of school and I made sure I moved as slowly as possible out of the classroom knowing I had to wait another 18 hours (yes, I had counted) until I could see him again... and then I heard it. His voice saying my name, and I turned to see him beckoning me towards him. I looked around to double check it was me he wanted but the corridor was deserted. It was me he wanted. I walked back into the classroom.

"Yes?" I said as he showed me to a seat in front of his desk.

"Oh, I just thought you worked very well today, despite the warning from your other teacher." I looked at him smiling, sweet of him. I still wanted to kiss him... and touch him...I put my bag down and looked up at him.

"Oh thank you, he just doesn't like me." I said twisting in the seat as his eyes were still on me.

"I don't see why, you're a beautiful..." he trailed off, his eyes widening at the slip of his tongue, and noticing he'd brought more attention to his mistake

"I mean well, um attractive and intelligent-"

"I think your sexy too." There. It came out of my mouth, just went whoosh, I had no control over what my tongue was doing alongside my vocal cords.

His mouth opened and closed, and he looked down , a smirk spreading across his mouth. He got up walking towards the classroom door and closing it and leaning against it with his arms crossed against his chest.

"Now, Lottie, you just did that thing, where you put a teacher like myself into a very dangerous situation." he looked up, the grin still there.

I had to have him. I really did. I could feel my pussy getting wet between my crossed legs, underneath my pleated skirt. I bit my lip.

"Oh, no don't be biting your lip...why are you doing that?" he said, a slightly pleading sound in his voice, but he couldn't tear his eyes away from me.

"Oh, I'm sorry sir, I didn't mean to offend you."

"You didn't" he said softly, I felt myself moving my

hand up my leg, inching my skirt up a bit so he could see my thigh.

"Lottie what are you doing?" he said moving forward slightly, he was clearly confused as to what he was going to do.

"Nothing." I said, innocently letting my skirt fold so it became shorter, making it look like an accident, even letting him glimpse my red french underwear...His eyes lit up.

"My first day... and you caught my attention immediately... and now you're trying to seduce me?" Steven said, looking at me with a hunger in his eyes. I looked at him, smiling slightly, trying not to be turned on, but I really was. He's a teacher, he would get in so much trouble if he got caught, but I wasn't stopping.

I stretched a little, pushing my chest out, making sure he looked at my breasts.

"Sir, what's wrong?" I said playfully. I looked down at his pants and I could see his hard dick pushing against the material. I gasped and he realised, strategically putting his hands on his crotch. I laughed.

"Why do you have to be so gorgeous?" his voice quiet as though he had gone shy... I looked up at him. I longed for him. Why was this attraction between us so sudden? I had never gotten like this before over anyone.

He clicked the lock on the door and I stood up, my heart beating hard against my chest.

I didn't know what to do, was he going to take me here in the classroom? Or was he going to send me home in embarrassment at even attempting to seduce a teacher? My mind raced alongside my heart which was thumping so hard against my chest. He walked towards me grabbing me by the shoulders so my lips were inches from his, he traced a finger along my full lips and a tingle went down my spine, he gripped my face in his hands and pushed his soft lips against mine. I moaned against his lips, pushing my body against his, grabbing onto his tie and pulling him deeper into the kiss. I felt his dick press against my hip and we both opened our eyes and I pulled away, becoming shy all of a sudden, but he soon changed my mind again.

Grabbing my body and kissing me frantically again he slipped his tongue into my mouth making me moan again as my tongue searched for his, to taste him again, his sweet taste. I then found my hands dragging themselves slowly up his body, un-tucking his shirt and running my fingers over his gorgeous skin, slightly moist with sweat as I pushed my hands over his muscles and towards his chest feeling every inch of his skin, he was panting leaning against me his eyes closed.

I kissed his lips again and his eyes snapped open as I took his hands and pushed them onto my breasts, I could feel my nipples harden under the lace of my bra. I gasped as he began to unbutton my shirt so I did the same to his, revealing the most gorgeous body I had ever seen. He was every inch perfect... I tugged at his tie and it slid to the floor, I gasped at his body. He was amazingly sexy.

He slung aside my shirt reaching around and unhooking my bra letting my breasts feel his breath and he licked them and kissed them.

He pulled me against him so my chest was against his, the feeling of his skin on mine was indescribable. I rubbed him through the material of his pants and he shuddered, I wanted him to touch me, I wanted him to make me come.

He picked me up and sat me on his desk hiking my skirt up so it sat neatly around my waist, leaving my French knickers on show. I blushed. I couldn't help but do so even though I was half naked something about being this exposed to this gorgeous man made my teenage body ache with shyness, and as though he had heard my thoughts he leaned forward and whispered

" I want you so much, please let me be inside you..."

I closed my eyes and nodded, this was like a dream, a lustful fantasy, a smile creeped across my lips as I slid my underwear down. He undid his trousers and let them drop, then only his tight boxers were left, leaving nothing to the imagination. I leaned forward sliding them down his muscled thighs and they dropped to the floor. He came closer to me, his dick throbbing, long hard and thick.

I couldn't wait to feel him inside me. He looked at me straight in the eye, like we did in class and I parted my legs so he could stand in between, where all the wetness was, he moved forward holding onto his hardness and guided it just to the entrance of my pussy, he began to slide the tip up and down my pussy lips, feeling all my wetness and making me even more turned on and he brushed against my clit, I moaned, so he did it again, my clit was swollen and sensitive and I gasped each time he rubbed his cock over it. Then he pulled away, I looked at him longingly and he thrust his fingers into me unexpectedly making me moan loudly. He kissed me to silence me as he thrust his fingers in and out of my tightness, my juices leaking onto the desk. He licked his fingers and licked his lips.

I blushed again, this intimacy with a stranger was so new to me. He leaned forward and whispered

" You taste so sweet..."

He moved forward again so his cock was at my tight hole again. I looked into his eyes and he smiled teasingly. I moaned in anticipation, I'd never seen a cock so big and was just desperate to feel him fill me. He pressed it so it slid inside me ever so slightly making me stiffen. Suddenly lust just took over me, I wanted him to fuck me hard immediately so I grabbed his arse cheeks and slammed him all the way inside me, his eyes widened as he let out a loud moan. So did I, his length filled me to the brink, I gasped as he stretched me. I moaned so loudly I covered my mouth, shaking with fear at the thought of someone discovering me with this gorgeous teacher but the longing for him making me go on.

He stayed still for a second or two, letting me get used to his size and he slid out of me making me gasp, then back in picking up the pace, I pulled his head towards me and moaned into his ear

" Please please fuck me..."

He stopped moving and looked down at me, he bit his lip as he looked my naked body up and down, his cock pulsing inside of me... He drew it out a little then... started fucking me hard. The wood surface of his desk sticking to the tops of my thighs and cheeks of my arse as I got sweatier, the desk rocking as he went deeper and deeper into me, knocking the breath out of me, his breath moist against my breasts, the smell of his aftershave and sweet sweat filling my nostrils. I pushed him away from me and he looked at me in desperation, I didn't want him to stop, but I wanted to be on top of him.

I pushed him to the floor and straddled his body

letting my wet pussy hover over him for a little while as the tingling sensations of sex subsided slightly, I lowered myself onto him and began to rock backwards and forwards, grinding against him, moans escaping his soft lips. I was in pure ecstasy... the feeling of him so deep inside me as he grabbed onto my hips and drove me harder down onto him.

I moaned and panted, sweat starting to roll down the valley between my bouncing breasts, my long hair sticking to my back.

I tossed my head back as he began to touch my clit with one hand while he massaged my left breast with the other. I gasped as he began to touch my clit faster making my pussy get wetter and wetter. I could feel myself begin to orgasm, the building up and rising of sensations until I couldn't keep it in anymore and my pussy clamped around his dick, he moaned loudly and shouted out "Ohhh fuck Lottie!" his voice filled with lust as he came at the same time as me, feeling him fill me with his juices. I moaned as wave after wave of pleasure took over my body, my sweet juices pouring from me over him and onto my thighs,until my I became too sensitive and I had to push myself from him, feeling our skin peel from each other and his dick slide out of me.

I was lying on my classroom floor with my gorgeous teacher, the cool of the floor making my back not want to peel away from it, but it did as he pulled me towards him so our naked bodies were pressed against eachn other. I looked at his face, his stubble rubbing against my soft cheek, the perfect manliness of him grasping me in his strong arms. I looked into his green eyes and was mesmerised. I smiled as our heart rates returned to normal, our chests pressed against one another. I kissed his lips and he returned it passionately as we embraced. He pulled away and shook his head and laughed and kissed me again.

"I never thought I'd fall for a student, in under two hours and have sex with her after class" he paused "Lottie?" I was so flattered that I didn't look away from his mouth as he spoke.

"Yeah?" I said, still panting slightly, my clit still throbbing between my legs.

"You are absolutely amazing...just wow."

"Steven, I want you too know, I'm not a slut. I've never done this before... with a teacher..." he raised a finger to my lips and shook his head, looking deep into my eyes he said softly

"No, I knew you weren't like that as soon as I saw you, only a special kind of girl attracts my eye." He kissed my forehead and I smiled and lay my head on his chest feeling that he was going to end this, making me feel like a stupid student. There was a moments silence, and then all the lights went out.

"Oh, they're locking up... Hmmm, I'm feeling a bit sweaty...you fancy a shower back at my place?"

I looked up at him, he was deadly serious... And I was in no way going to refuse...

THE CHECK-UP
Doctor and Patient

The medical doctor opens up the door to one of his hospital rooms located in the very back and sees a female patient sitting on the table waiting for him ready for her checkup.

The doctor then quickly locks the door and then smiles at her because this is his favorite and hottest patient.

The woman returns his smile because he is her favorite doctor.

The doctor drools over the womans clear porcelain skin, big blue eyes and long mane of golden blonde hair.

The woman patient possesses quite a body too!

She has endless white creamy legs, 36-inch accomodating hips, a fantastic shapely ass, a slim and curvy 22 inch waist, and is the very proud owner of an amazing all natural 50GG bosom with wide areole and big pink nipples, which is totally untouched by any plastic surgeons hands.

The doctor smiles, his cock immedietly springing to life, as he then tells his patient it's checkup time as he instructs the lady to take off all her clothes.

The doctor drools as he watches the voluptous woman reach in back off her as she unzips the back of her white outfit down. As soon as she does so the outfit falls to the ground.

Then the doctor watches as the woman starts to unclasp her enormous bra, which is bulging with tit flesh.

As soon as the woman takes off her bra her gargantuan, round melons pop out excitedly, happy to be free from its confining harnass, filling up the whole hospital room!

The doctor feels his dick get even harder as she raises both legs at him and instructs him to pull off her panties and sandal high heeled shoes for her.

The doctor then quickly takes off her left sandal high heeled shoe and then her right one as he then quickly reaches down towards her hips and yanks her panties right off of her.

The lady totally naked now smiles sexily at the doctor as she strikes a very sexy pose for him, shimmying her giant breasts and crossing her shapely long legs.

The doctor going wild over his hot patients teasing quickly gets nude too.

As soon as the doctor takes off his last piece of clothing , which is his underwear, his monster dick pops out excitedly happy to be free from its confining place.

The doctor, his dick getting harder and harder by the second, then starts to examine his patient by taking out his stethescope and putting it against her mammoth chest to check her heartbeat.

The doctor tells his woman patient her heart is A-ok as he reaches over and fondles her bountiful breasts making her giggle excitedly.

The doctor then gets out his little hammer and instructs the woman to cross her legs as she immedietly crosses her right leg over her left one.
In doing so her right foot brushes against The doctor's already very excited cock, making it pulse even more in excitement.

The doctor then taps her right knee with the little hammer making the womans right foot jump up excitedly brushing against his massive cock again.

After the doctor finds her right leg A-ok he then instructs his patient to cross her left leg over her right as she quickly does so, flashing off her succulent pussy, as her left foot now brushes excitedly against his cock.

The doctor then taps her left knee with the hammer as the womans left foot jumps up brushing against his cock still again.

The voluptous lady then looks at the doctor laughing as the doctor looks and drools at all the amazing super- stacked quivering titflesh she possesses.

The lady not through with her teasing just yet then lifts her left foot again and gives the doctor's mighty cock a hard tug down with her foot.
The instant she does this the doctor has to use all his will power not to cum all over the fucking hospital floor.

After succeding in not ejaculating just yet the very horny doctor tells his female patient that her left leg is A-ok too.

The doctor then tells his voluptous female patient that she is in great shape as the woman then jumps happily up into the doctors arms straddling him, with her arms around his neck and her legs straddling his back.

The doctor holding up the female patient off the ground now enters his one eyed monster into her all too willing pussy as he then starts to fuck her.

Up and down vigorously the woman goes on the doctors cock as they soon reach an earth shatterring orgasm at the same time and come in one massive shudder.

The doctor then puts his favorite female patient down to the ground as she then climbs up on the examination table and sticks her very shapely ass in his direction as she wiggles it sexily at him and orders him to fuck her royally doggy style.

The woman does not have to ask her horny doctor twice as he jumps on the table with her as he first licks her sweet pussy with his talented tongue as he then starts to fuck the living daylights out of her!

The very beautiful, stacked woman makes the most dick hardening erotic cries of lust as she is being fucked by her doctor as she soon explodes in explosive orgasm over and over and over again.

It does not matter if the doctor is 50 years old to her 25, his monster dick is second to none, as it does it's work between her pussy lips.

Soon the doctor joins his favorite female patient as he explodes happily with her in earth shatterring orgasm.

The woman not done yet then takes her doctors mammoth cock into her sweet mouth and sucks him off to another mighty erection as she then instructs her doctor to bang her sweet ass!
The doctor not wasting a second then takes a deep breath and puts his horse sized monster dong inside her super tight shit hole!

The womans shit hole is so tight it makes the doctor cum soon, very wildly and excitedly inside of her.

The woman patient, totally filled up by such a monstous cock coming inside of her soon comes wildly too!

The woman like a bitch in heat then takes the doctor's mammoth cock between her lips again and sucks him off to still another incredible erection as she then instructs him to cum all over her mountainous melons, as she takes his cock and puts it right between her twin hemispheres of flesh.

With all the wonderful friction of her huge,pillowy tit's against his cock the doctor soon loses total control and orgasms mightily all over his favorite female patient mammoth mammaries.

The lady then shares a laugh with her doctor as she washes the doctors cum all over her giant bosom.

The doctor and his favorite and hottest female patient then start to put on their clothes again.

Once they get their clothes back on they start to kiss each other very passionately.

"See you next week for another checkup doctor?" the sexy female patient asks sweetly looking up at his face.

"Sure thing honey and I must say that you are one very hot, young sexy wife!" the doctor replies smiling as he gives his wifes fleshy, firm shapely buttcheeks a pat making her moan pleasurably, as she rushes out the door as the doctor waits for his next patient to arrive!

THE REUNION

The Cheerleader and The Soldier

I am standing in line at the bar, waiting to order a beer. How I talked myself into coming to my high school reunion was beyond me. I disliked most of the people here when I was in school, and not too much had changed. Most haven't done anything with their lives. Here I stand, nearly 28 years old, a highly decorated Navy Seal, second in my class at the Naval Academy, and newly promoted to Lieutenant Commander. What a waste of time this turned out to be.

It doesn't help much that I am wearing my full dress uniform, my medals reflecting in the light from the strobes. Muscle bound, head shaved, I guess I am a little impressive, and with the nasty shrapnel scar on the side of neck, a bit scary.

In she walks: Anna Fraser. I haven't seen her since graduation. She was off to Harvard, and I was off to the Navy. We had lots in common, I was the star running back on the football team, and she the cheerleader. We are both brilliant, she graduated valedictorian; me salutatorian, both only 17. For some reason, we never got together. There was always some sparks between us, but nothing ever happened, although I would have given my left nut to get inside her. She is dressed in her old cheerleading uniform, along with the rest of her old squad. I caught myself staring. Her uniform still fits quite well. The blue sweater is tighter, but it looks better that way. It seems to accentuate her beautiful firm C cups. Her skirt rides high on her hips, the waist almost bursting from her womanly hips, the hem barely reaching mid-thigh. Her hair is tied back in a cute ponytail. The memories come flooding back. Her milky thighs high-kicking at games, her firm and perky tits bouncing, glimpses of panties, imagining all of the things I could do to her, all of the things she could do to me.

She is stopped not far from the door, having being noticed by the faculty. One of her favorite teachers starts up a conversation with her. I stare at her again, all my old insecurities coming to the surface, but being in the Seals has changed a few things in me. I order a second beer, and sum up my courage, and walk towards her.

I purposely position myself so she can see me striding confidently towards her. Her eyes trail down my body, sizing me up. I can tell she is intrigued. Her warm smile greets me as I close the distance between us. She still has those cute dimples. She greets me with a cute giggle, and jumps up hugging me, throwing her arms around my neck, her legs wrapping around mine. I am instantly hard.

Still holding the two bottles, I am unable to return the bear hug. Finally, she reluctantly releases me. I lean down to her and kiss her on the cheek, handing her a bottle. Coors Light, always her favorite. She looks and the bottle, her face splitting to a wide smile. "You still remember, after all these years?"

"I never forget what a beautiful woman drinks." I return the smile, sipping at my beer.

"Always the charmer. And I see you are the big, tough, successful soldier."

"Lieutenant Commander James Liam Dove, United States Navy, at your service."

"So Commander, are you going to ask me to dance?" Anna says with a sexy smile, tossing back the last of her beer. Not waiting for an answer, she grabs me by the hand, leading me onto the floor.

Dancing and grinding to the pumping rhythm, I am getting extremely fired up. Anna is rubbing herself all over me, and she is wet. Her body is face is flushed, the redness leading all the way down her chest, past the neck of her sweater. The few strands of hair which have escaped her ponytail are matted and stuck to her forehead. Beads of sweat are trailing down her neck, her skin shining. Her chest is heaving, her breathing labored. She looks likes a goddess, completely immersing herself in the moment.

Her cheerleader uniform is painting the picture of an innocent schoolgirl, but with the scent of a sexual predator. I myself am nearly out of breath, and my raging cock feels like it will tear its way out of my uniform slacks. Finally, mercifully, the song ends. I cup her chin and kiss her deeply. My hands roaming their way down her back, caressing the taut globes of her ass.

She presses her body hard into mine, her hands rubbing my back.

"Get me out of here. Take me away. Please. Take me somewhere, anywhere but here, please." Anna sighed as I finally released her from the body kiss.

I hold her hand tight, weaving our way through the crowd towards the hallway. I lead her down the hall towards the parking lot, but Anna has other ideas. She pushes open the door to the Nurses Office. "I'm sick... I need some medicine."

After getting through the door, she attacks me. I barely keep standing as she kisses and grinds against me.

I reach down and grab the edge of her sweater, pulling it quickly over her head. The saucy little tart isn't wearing a bra.

I step back, pulling off my uniform jacket, letting her start to undo the buttons on my shirt. I undo my pants, dropping them to the floor, leaving me naked.

I turn Anna around, pressing her against the wall; her tits pressing against the wall, nipples crushed flat by our body weight, clad only in her tight skirt. I kiss her across her neck and down her back. She is moaning in delight. My rock hard member is pressed into her ass. My fingers find their way to her dripping pussy. I quickly find her nub, rubbing and caressing it gently, two fingers plunging deep.

I'm enjoying the feel of her body twitching in reaction of my manipulations. More and more, I tease her. She is leaking like a faucet now on my hand. Her breathing is coming in short, loud gasps, echoing in the small room.

After a few minutes of my torturous fondling of her body, she spins around, dropping to her knees. She engulfs my raging cock, her tongue swirling in her mouth. My hands find their way to her hair, fingers entangling themselves in her golden locks. I tilt my head back, mouth open; the sensations overwhelming.

She seems to be enjoying this almost as much as I am. I don't want this to end, but I am getting close. I don't want to waste myself in her mouth. I reach under her chin, pushing up gently. She releases me reluctantly.

Spying the empty desk, I bend her over, burying myself into her in one deep, powerful thrust. She is squealing like a cat in heat. She is pushing herself back on my hard cock, our hips slamming together on every shot. My hands reached around her, cupping her breasts, fingers tweaking her nipples.

Anna flailed her head around wildly as her squeals became full throated screams. She was getting off unlike anything I have ever seen before.

Anna still keeps fucking back at me after her orgasm subsides, turning her head and whispering, "Is the big handsome football player going to satisfy his dirty cheerleader before going off to the war?"

"What does the dirty little cheerleader want?"

She pushes off the desk, and leads me to the cot. She has me lay down on the cot, and climbs nimbly on top. In one fluid motion, she imbeds herself on me. She bounces wildly on top of me, grabbing my hands and roughly grinds them into her breasts. Her radiant skin is shiny with moisture, the sweat just pouring out of her now. Her hair is soaked, light makeup running, but she is still beautiful.

Looking up at her riding me like a cowgirl, I couldn't hold out much more. She hammered down on my body; I forced myself up, banging her tight, little body harder than I though she could take.

Our bodies slammed so hard together that it sounded like I was spanking her, spanking her extremely hard and fast. Anna pushed her hand between her legs and started rubbing her clit. I could tell that she was getting close to coming again. Her moans became louder and more unrestrained.

"Oh, Jesus!" She screamed. "Give me everything you've got."

She didn't need to ask me twice. I let loose a torrent in her and hollered out a loud moan.

She collapses on top of me; her body seemingly in the midst of an epileptic seizure. We lay still for a few moments before I removed myself from her. I ran my cock over her bush, leaving a trail of my seed over her mound.

I leaned forward and kissed her, having never appreciated her so much. "That was great,"

"Thank you," she replied, "After all these years; I finally got laid by you. The football star, turned into the great hero."

I just smiled at her, holding her close. "Strange how things work out. I wasn't even going to come to this reunion. I thought it would be a waste of time."

She just smiled and kissed me.

I would like to invite you to read another one of my books that I think you will really enjoy. The book is called:

"FILTHY SEXY STORIES FOR ADULTS:
10 Short Exciting and Spicy Stories"

Enjoy!

WELCOME HOME
Bondage Bdsm Story

You come home from work and find me waiting for you. I am wearing a French maid uniform with white thigh highs and black stiletto heels. I lead you to the bathroom where a robe and toiletries are ready for you. Relaxing music is playing.

"We have about half an hour until dinner is ready, Sir."

You take a long hot shower after your night at work and find your favorite shampoos and soaps waiting for you. You find me in the kitchen preparing dinner. I turn and smile,

"We have a few minutes until dinner if you would like to watch TV. I made you a rum and coke. It is in by the couch."

You smile and lean down to kiss the back of my neck, knowing that it makes my pussy instantly wet.

"What are we having, hun?"

"Grilled steaks, with sautéed mushrooms and onions. Twice baked potatoes and a Mediterranean salad. For dessert strawberry short cake."

I feel your hands brushing up my legs, pulling my skirt up to reveal my black lace boy shorts. I lean back into you and you pull my hair to turn my head, kissing me hard; your tongue chasing mine. I break away from you.

"Sir, if you keep distracting me dinner will be ruined. Please have a drink and relax."

I smile at you.

You leave me in the kitchen and find a tv tray in the living room with the remote and a drink sitting by your favorite chair. A few minutes later I bring in our dinner. We eat and discuss our day while you search the TV for some entertainment. After we have eaten, I take your dishes,

"Sir, if you go lay on the bed it is time for your massage."

You look at me as though you are going to argue, but I am off to the kitchen putting the dishes in the washer and cleaning the kitchen. You walk to the bedroom to find candles lit, fresh sheets on the bed, music playing and oil sitting by the bed. You lie down on your back and start to drift with the music. I come into the room and start with a light massage of your head and face, working down to your arms, and then your legs. I use long slow strokes to relax your body. Then I sit at the end of the bed and use a vanilla lotion to massage your feet.

"Have you ever had your feet rubbed babe?" I ask you softly.

But you can only moan. I help you roll over on to your stomach and work the back of your legs and your back, making sure to stretch out your lower back and sciatic area, running my fingernails lightly across your back. As I finish your massage I lean down and whisper in your ear

"Anything else you want, Sir?"

You moan 'yes', and before I can react you grab me and pull me down under you, pinning me to the bed. You kiss me and run your hands down my body feeling the satin of the maid outfit. You can feel my lacy bra and your hand runs down my stomach to my lacy panties. You rub my clit and I moan into your mouth as your tongue teases mine. You lean back and smile at me.

"Yes, there is something I want", and you pull out a set of silk ties. "Remember what we talked about this morning?"

I nod yes.

"Tell me what you want," you say to me.

I blush. "I want you to tie me up, shave my pussy, and tease and fuck me until I beg you to stop."

You smile at me and raise my hands above my head tying them to the bed and then move to the end of the bed and tie my legs spread eagle to the bed. You place a pillow under me to raise me up off the bed and lay a towel down and bring warm water, saving cream, and a razor from the bathroom. I am squirming with anticipation. You place your hand on my stomach, right above my hips, to stop my moving. With the other hand you pull the black lacy panties down my legs and pull them over my feet. You spread a thin layer of saving cream over my pussy. I close my eyes and feel your warm hands gliding over my body. A few moments later I feel the razor slowly take the first strip off of my pussy.

"You ok babe?" you ask me.

I nod my head 'yes', unable to speak. You continue to shave me until my pussy is soft and naked. You use the warm water with a washcloth and clean off the remaining shaving cream. The warmth makes me moan. You slip a finger into my pussy and I try to sit up to look at you, but the ties hold me to the bed. You slowly pull your finger out of me while my muscles and hips try to pull you back in. I moan in protest and you lean up to look me in the eye.

"Baby you need to behave or I will blindfold you," you say to me, trying to look stern.

"Yes Sir," I pout.

You stand up and walk out of the room. I start to protest and you give me a look that tells me I really shouldn't. I lay there waiting, listening to the music I turned on for your massage and slowly I relax, forgetting that I am even tied to the bed, naked and under your control. You return to the room with a box, of what I can only assume contains the objects you have been thinking about using on me all day.

"I am going to blindfold you hun, I know you have behaved, but I want you to feel everything." My eyes widen but I don't say anything to you. The wetness on my thighs tells you everything. You place the large black blindfold over my eyes. I feel you slide your hand under me and unzip the maid's uniform and pull from my body. I can feel your eyes running down my body. From my black lacy bra that holds my tits up high, down to my white thigh highs and heels. You put your box of tricks on the bed, so that they are close to us at bra and pull it up my arms, so that I am naked for you. Then you tie my arms again.

I suck in air as I feel an ice cube tracing around my left nipple and then slowly run over to trace my right nipple as well. The cold makes them stand at attention. Your warm tongue flicks over my left nipple as the ice trails slowly around the right. You suck the nipple into your mouth and my back arches towards you.

"Hun, if you misbehave like that again I will have to punish you and I don't want to have to do that." You whisper up to me, returning to work on my tits.

My body is on fire and it is taking everything in me not to move. The ice moves down my chest as your mouth moves on to the right nipple. You bite me slightly, knowing it makes my pussy wet to be bitten. Then, your tongue follows the ice down my body until you place it on my clit.

"Ahhh, God," I can't stop myself from moaning.

You smile knowing how hard it is for me to give up control and how hot and wet it is making me.

You slip the ice cube into my pussy while you lick my clit. My body jerks at the cold of the ice and the heat of your mouth. Your mouth leaves me to place soft kisses around my pussy, but never on my clit which is where my body is begging for you to touch me. Your finger holds the ice inside my pussy while it melts. You can feel my muscles squeezing at the cold ice and at your finger. You move down so that you are between my legs and my soaked pussy is raised and exposed for your every desire. You lick me, from the cool wetness leaking out of me, up to my clit where you suck hard. I lean my head back and moan aloud. You reach into the box taking out one of my vibrators and slowly slide it into my tight, wet pussy. Watching it open up to envelope the toy that is a just a bit smaller than the size of your own throbbing cock.

I have no idea how you are keeping control, as you slowly turn the knob of the vibrator on until is it as high as it goes.

"UUHHH please," I moan.

"Please, what hun? You ask. "Please fuck my baby?"

 I beg.

"No hun, I am not done with you yet. I know you can take more than this." You slowly start fucking me with the vibrator. My breathing is getting heavier by the second and your thrusts become quicker and you watch my pussy squeeze tight, trying to hold on to the vibrating cock. I start to whimper and you know I can't take this speed much more. You pull the toy from me, returning it to the box. I am lost in darkness my pussy
yearning at the air, longing to find any part of you.

"AGGGHHH fuck!"

I feel hot wax drizzle across my tits. Just as I calm

down another drizzle onto my belly. My body quivers. You use one hand to spread my pussy juices down to my ass, while the other hand removes the wax from my body. Each time your finger grazes my asshole my hips buck.

You lean up and remove the blindfold, kissing me deeply and letting me suck on your tongue. My body is on fire and I want you so badly right now. I will let you do anything. You know this. You roll so that you are between my legs as we kiss. I feel your hard cock against my pussy. I sigh softly and you push your cock all the way into my pussy in one hard thrust while you cover my mouth with your own. I moan into your mouth. Your cock is tight in my little pussy and it drives me crazy. My hands are clenched above our heads and my breathing is short and shallow. You lean back so you can look at my face.

Slowly you start shallow thrusting into my pussy, the muscles melting around your cock, molding it to your desire.

"That's it. Let me take you Destiny."

As your thrusts become quicker and more urgent, my moans become louder. You pull your cock almost all the way out of my pussy and slam it back in. It feels so good that I haven't noticed that you have untied my hands from the headboard and tied them together behind your neck.

"Ahhh, yes fuck me hard, ahhh, please baby," I beg you.

You thrust faster than ever and I can feel your cock growing just a little inside of me. I know you are going to come and I am about to come too. You pull my feet free from the ties, and roll me over onto my stomach. I feel you pull my hips up to you and your cock sinks back into my pussy. From the box of tricks you find my small glass dildo and tease my ass with it slowly pushing it in.

"It's....so....tight....I'm gonna cum...oh...please."

I can feel you balls slapping against my clit and your hand drive the dildo into my ass in time with each thrust of your cock. You slap my ass hard and my muscles contract around your cock and don't loosen up.

"Oh ......fuck.....yes" I scream. Your hot breath is on the back of my neck.

"Come with me," you yell and slap my ass again.

My pussy oozes all over your balls and you shoot my pussy full of your cum in three more thrusts. We collapse on our sides with you and the dildo still inside of me. My thigh highs are drenched and we cannot move; for a long time we breathe more and more softly.

You finally lean forward and kiss the back of my

neck. "Mmm. I should call you sir more often."

I giggle.

BUZZING FEMDOM

Femdom Bsm Story

John inserted the key into his front door as quietly as he could. He slipped inside, putting his laptop case down ever so gently, and closed his eyes for a moment. Oh, hello you! There she was, padding barefoot down the stairs. She did not come to him; she stopped three steps up, so that her womanly pubis was level with his mouth, so that he had to look up to her, almost look up her. Today she had on a plain black cotton t-shirt and a plain black cotton miniskirt. He knew that under the skirt would be plain white cotton knickers. At the height she stood they were a hair's breadth from being visible to him.

Sandra's soft brown eyes looked at John. The urgent feminine greed he saw there unnerved him now as it did every evening when he returned home. Her lips were parted, her slim body faced his, her face was tilted down and her straight, shoulder length hair swung forward a little. There were no words, but her plea was loud and clear. Come upstairs with me now. Come up and give me what I need. Now. Right now.

In the bedroom Sandra undressed him with practiced and efficient grace. Short-sleeved shirt, tie. With submissive obedience he lifted each foot so she could remove his shoes, socks and trousers. She did not hurry, but he felt her anticipation, her delayed gratification. It had become a ritual of helplessness for him, each step taking away the need for him to participate, each devotional act confirming his passive role. She knelt before him and slowly pulled down his briefs. He was already made hard by the anticipation of his wife's attentions and their inevitable outcome. Now he stood naked and erect. Utterly submissive.

As part of her ceremonial preparation Sandra washed John's genitals. She used a soft flannel soaked in cool water with a dash of lemon-scented bath oil. He knew she had learned to take her time because any sense of pressure or urgency would reduce his output. He knew that from this point and for the next few hours her sole aim was to make him come as many time as he was able, and for each pulsing orgasm to produce as much semen as possible. Their physical relationship had turned from something sexual and mutual into something parasitic. No, not parasitic, because parasites took from their hosts and gave nothing back. This was symbiosis. She took his creamy fluid, all he could manage, and in return she gave him orgasms, through the evening and into the night, leaving him in a state of dizzy, throbbing exhaustion that had become addictive for him.

At first, as he realised what was happening to them, John had tried to turn the ceremony back to what had been before, something more normal. He would reach for her knickers, roll over on top of her, kiss her nipples. But each time, with beautiful, gentle authority, she guided him back to her path, led him to her needs. And, oh, how he would succumb. Succumb. It was the perfect word for what he did. He was sucked; he would come. She would suck, until he came again. Suck. Come. Suck. Come.

When he asked her why, she told him it was what she wanted. When he wondered if it was what he wanted his throbbing, aching member betrayed him, playing stupid, helpless slave to the mastery of her cunning lips. A masculine glimmer of rebellion flashed through him, as it often did at this stage, just before the relentless sucking started. He had the impulse to kneel down, pull her up to her feet, hold her, kiss her, undress her, fuck with her. With. Together. But she always seemed to sense this moment and her soothing, teasing massage would slow and intensify, stroking away his impulse and his will.

His role was to be sucked. At this moment it was what he wanted too. As he relaxed he could feel his cock harden even more, and his moment of uncertainty would melt away under Sandra's cool, wet rubbing and his own surging need for release. He lay back on the bed with his breath catching in his throat. She tied his wrists to the bedhead. She had learned that this excited him, increased his capacity. She lay down next to him smiling and looked lovingly at him. Was it love? He let this final flit of worry dance into the shadows and closed his eyes. He was strong and fit, but he needed to save all his athletic prowess for what was to come. He felt her hair brush lightly but deliciously over his thighs. Her delicate fingers closed around his bulging cock and began to slide his foreskin back and forth in slow, gentle strokes.

In the six months since the sucking had first started John had gone through several stages of wonder and disbelief at how good Sandra had become at doing the things she did to him. All his previous experience of being masturbated by a woman, including her, was a mix of pain and dissatisfaction. They would push down too hard on his foreskin, hold his cock too low down, go too fast, squeeze too hard, keep changing hands. The worst times were when they stopped stroking, as if caught by surprise at his ejaculation.

But driven by her need to express and taste his fluid, Sandra had learned well. Her fingers curled around his cock an inch from his tip, sliding his foreskin slowly back and forth over the helmet of his penis. She did not push it down all the way, her strokes were just long enough to stretch his sliding skin over the base of his helmet and then back up almost, but not quite, to his tip. She started with thumb and forefinger curled around his hot shaft, a gentle but insistent rhythm, two or three strokes a second.

He knew she would not stop or vary this perfect, delicious motion until she made him come. The certainty of her relentless stroking allowed him to slip into semi-consciousness. As he surrendered carelessly into erotic catatonia his breathing slowed. The bed bounced softly as her hand worked its up and down magic on his rock hard shaft. He was getting close now, his breaths deepening, and he felt that lovely, involuntary physical sensation of fluid flowing in his balls, moving, filling tubes and pipes, waiting to explode out of his body and into her sweet, sweet mouth. He felt her lips close gently around his tip and, without disturbing the slow, pistoning rhythm of her hand, they began to suck him. He knew that she spent a lot of her day at home working out, strengthening her muscles and her breathing while she waited eagerly for his return.

Each time now it felt that her sucking was becoming more intense. Tonight it was almost too much and he gasped as he felt the force of her oral suction on the end of his cock, as if she was going to suck him inside out. Her hot saliva lubricated his throbbing tip, ensuring a perfect suction seal that was so strong he could feel the end of his penis expand inside her mouth and sense the blood being pulled into his shaft making it even harder and longer. It was erotically primitive, this sense of something, someone, her, her mouth, wanting, needing, demanding, sucking, feeding, pulling, drawing his fluids out of him and into her. Her tongue caressed his bulging helmet inside her hot, wet mouth and he succumbed. Completely. Oh, fuck. Oh, fuck. Thick, hot gouts, spurting, squirting deep into her, trying to fulfil, trying to sate. Great pulses of pleasure coursed through his loins, surging more and more of his creaminess up his throbbing shaft and discharging it over her honey sweet tongue, into her eager, swallowing throat. He came and came, gave her everything he had. Oh, fuck. Oh, fuck! When will it stop?

He was panting, sucking in great gulps of air. His head was spinning and his vision sparkled as the world seemed to tip and sway with the shuddering intensity of his endless climax. As his euphoric insanity cleared he sensed her final savouring and swallowing of him, heard her sigh, felt her lips open and move down his still pulsing cock, sucking and licking, slowly and firmly, making sure they did not lose a single drop. She too was breathing hard, giving little shivers of delight against him. It felt like a deeper need, beyond sex. He didn't want to understand it. Perhaps she didn't either. But she indulged herself in that need, submerged herself in it totally, and she was pulling him in with her.

Sandra left John for a few minutes. When she came back she had a glass of orange juice and a bowl of yoghurt. She did not untie his hands. Instead she help the glass to his lips and then fed him with a spoon. He drank and ate everything. It reinforced his obedient submission. It occurred to him that apart from her greeting when he had arrived from work, the only words uttered between them were his vocal ejaculations as he came. He opened his mouth, as if to attempt conversation. Several times he had wanted to ask if she put something in the drink, something that helped him come so many times. But this too now seemed unimportant. What mattered was how many times. He swallowed his final mouthful and she leaned forward to kissed his lips, leaving a wasteful glaze of his semen on them. Her big brown eyes looked into his and he gave her what she was seeking, total acceptance of her need, total surrender to her ordeal by oral sex. Yes, he was ready for her.

Without a word she climbed over him and faced down the bed so that her knees were either side of his head, resting against his shoulders. He looked up her short skirt at her white knickers. They were a few inches from his mouth. He wanted to reach up and kiss them but his hands were tied and he knew he had to remain still and passive. Only when she sensed his complete calm would she open her knees and let her hot gusset press against his mouth. It was another discovery, his powerful sexual response to being smothered by her panties. Through weeks of learning they had found that simple, white cotton worked best. Simple white cotton always made him come again. Her hot, cotton covered sex pressed against his open mouth and his nose. He had to strain to breathe and each struggling inhalation drew into him the sense and the spicy smell of her gently squirming vagina. His questing, tasting tongue rasped against the hot dryness of the fabric, moistening, oiling, so he could better feel the outline of her vulva as it rocked across his mouth.

He was helplessly erect. Again he felt her hair brush against his thighs and again he gasped as her mouth slid slowly over his helmet enclosing it in her wet, irresistible vacuum which only he could fill. Her hand was already pumping his hard shaft, gliding up and down with exquisite relentlessness. He opened his legs and, at this invitation, she moved her other hand which now clasped his testicles and began a gentle, pulsing squeezing. It was an erotically merciless interrogation that always produced his liquid confession; the only question was when.

Now. Oh. Now. I confess. And it hurts, it hurts. His loins thrust up towards her as his fluid jetted into her mouth once more. His aching muscles spasmed with waves of joy and release. His cries of agonised fulfilment were muffled under her genital gag. He strained to take huge, smothered intakes of breath that were laden with the hot smell of her sex. He was blacking out as the final, desperate gouts of his semen left him for her. The cocktail surge of depleted oxygen, ecstasy and pain drained him of his feeling of self. Who was he? He didn't care. He didn't even know.

Slowly he recovered. Hormones of arousal bubbled in his blood and the euphoria of such intense release simplified his reality. He was to be sucked. He wanted to be sucked. She must suck him again. Now she took her panties off and, with the same waiting for his breathing to slow, the same patience, she lowered herself onto his mouth again. A third arousal so soon after orgasm might be painful which is why she kept the lubricant in the fridge. He felt soothing coldness squirt over his hot, throbbing penis. Eased by the cool, slippery jelly, her hand moved differently, sliding up and down the full length of his exhausted cock. The intense taste of her womanhood sliding over his mouth together with the inevitability of her interrogating hands forced his response. He hardened slowly, but she knew how to rebuild his resolution. Cold jelly squirted against him again. It was so soothing and lovely, allowing her hand to move up and down faster and faster, making her body bounce and thrust against his mouth. His tongue twirled inside her, tasting her juices as she too became aroused. Now he needed to sense her excitement in order to give her the answer she needed. Now she started to come, great sobbing cries of joy as his tongue licked and curled against her pulsing, shivering clitoris.

Afterwards, if he remembered, he might wonder how she had become so multi-orgasmic, for this was new as well. In the old days she would lose interest after the first one. Now she was insatiable. Or had she learned that this was the best way to make him produce another orgasm so quickly? Was she faking it just to get what she needed from him? But increasingly he did not remember or wonder. Increasingly she was reducing him to a state of emptied fulfilment that left no desire or space for thought.

Her wet, thrusting vagina smothered him, filling him with another divine cocktail of panic and arousal. Again he felt her lips close over him. Again he felt her suck, harder still this time, the vacuum so strong he could feel it forcing the fluid out of his balls. Again he climaxed, her lips clamped round him and accepting his gouting discharge into her mouth as if she was part of his cock, as if her whole being was a sucking, swallowing extension of his sexuality. Now it felt right, the inevitability of her need and what it meant to them, to him. Now he felt himself being immersed in her obsession, floating away in it, carried by her along a river of orgasmic oblivion that had no end.

Sandra left John a little longer this time. When she returned she had her iPod and some electric toys that she would use on him to ensure his complete emptying. She slipped the headphones onto him and saw a new look in his eyes. There was wonder. There was love mixed with confusion. He felt as if she was gradually sucking him away, swallowing his masculinity, his very meaning. He looked at her beautiful mouth. Her lips were full and soft, inviting him to come inside. Again and again. To perform his role. To be sucked. To feed her mouth with his body. His cock jerked upright as if woken from a dream, as if it was disconnected from him; leaving him so it could spend the rest of its life inside her warm, nurturing mouth, carrying out its own selfish purpose of taking his ever diminishing essence and delivering it into her hot, sucking desire. He felt a final surge of fear, as of a man who realises he is becoming insane, just before the madness steals him away.

There, there. She kissed him lightly on the lips. Her reassurance was wordless. Don't worry. I won't hurt you; I only want one thing from you. That's all I want.

And it's all you want too. Shhh. The stroking and buzzing and sucking went on for hours. At some point deep in the night he whispered hoarsely that he could not come any more. But, as they always did, her clever lips found a way, sucked a little harder. Until he was gone.

SABRINA WILL

Spanking Bdsm Story

Fresh out of college I took a job at a marketing firm on Madison Avenue, making terrible wages and working for a terrible boss. Her name was Sabrina Sexton, and for a while I thought she was actually insane.

It wasn't that she worked us hard, if you're young and ambitious enough to go to NYC for a job you expect to be worked hard. Instead, at times she seemed schizophrenic. She'd heap praise on me in the morning and the scream at me in the afternoon. She'd tell me what she wanted, and after I had followed her instructions to the letter, she'd threaten to fire me for wasting the company's time on bullshit.

Of course employees talk, and we certainly talked about her. When I speculated she was literally crazy, someone else suggested she had a problem with amphetamines. In all cases we weren't sure how she managed to first get her job, and then keep it.

Some of us expected she must have slept with the big boss. Sabrina was smoking hot, even for a woman 15 years older than me. Single and no kids so she spent a good deal of her free time at the gym. At least, when she talked about off time, that's what she talked about.

She was average height, about 5'5" with a fit body that had just the right slope from her waist to her hips. Her hair was chestnut brown, but it was difficult to tell how long it was because she always wore it up revealing an elegant neck. Her glasses gave her a bit of that sexy librarian vibe.

Still despite being meticulously put together, she seemed a mess. She had talent for the marketing world, there was no doubt about that, but she was not a leader. We succeeded as a team in spite of her.

One day, in the middle of a preparing for a big client presentation, I had had computer troubles and the IT guys had screwed around and robbed me of a few hours of my life. So when everyone else was leaving for home, I was stuck finishing my end of the product.

My friend Charlie, a well-manicured Latino who I'm pretty sure was gay patted me on the back and smiled, "You sure you want to be alone here with the bitch?

Who knows what she'll do with only one person to scream at." Sabrina was still in her office, a glass encased box on one side of the room, but she kept the blinds drawn.

I laughed and said, "I'm gonna have to brave it, Charlie. If you don't see me tomorrow tell my parents I love them." He laughed as he made his way to the elevator.

Sure enough about 20 minutes later, Sabrina's door opened and she looked around the office, confused at its emptiness. When her eyes fixed on me, they narrowed and she barked, "You. Get in here. Now."

"Great," I thought to myself, "Thanks IT." But I dutifully made my way toward her office and walked in.

"Close the door," she ordered. When I started to say there was no need since we were alone she cut me off and through gritted teeth she said, "A simple goddamn order and you can't even do that without 50 fucking complaints."

I rolled my eyes to myself as I shut the door. Trying to maintain a pleasant disposition in order to end this meeting quickly I said, "So Ms. Sexton, what can I do for you?"

"For starters you can redo all of the copy on the recent campaign," she said tossing a file of paper work at me.

"Um," I started taken aback, "I'm a graphic artist, not a copy writer."

"So you don't know how to write fucking English?" She insulted me. "You went to college, didn't you? Surely your degree made you take writing classes."

I didn't really know what to say, "Well, I could try, but I still have to finish the graphics we decided on, and that will take me a while."

"Jesus Christ," she muttered, "Useless, all of you are fucking useless."

It was the end of a long day so I said the first thing that came to mind, "So why don't you just do it yourself then?" It was part frustration, part serious suggestion. I mean, what did she do all day?

She looked a little stunned. "You know what," she said, "Just go home, and don't bother coming back tomorrow."

I shouted, "Are you fucking kidding me?" I needed this job, but I wasn't about to beg for it. "You know what Sabrina, you don't fucking deserve me or anyone else who works in this office."

Her eyes went wide and then narrowed in anger, but I continued, "If you look good to the big boss it's only because people like me work hard despite your so-called leadership. You soak up the praise and the paycheck, but don't deserve shit. You're like a spoiled child and you should be treated like one."

She laughed at me and mocked, "What does that mean? Are you going to spank me?"

The frustration with her and this job took over as I stepped to her, my 6'0 frame dwarfing her own. I all but snarled, "Someone should."

"Like you're man enough," she said sarcastically, but there was a kind of wide-eyed hunger inspired by my aggression. I took her roughly by the back of the neck and pushed her forward over her desk. She whimpered at the rough treatment as I made her bend at the waist.

"What do you think you're doing?" She breathed huskily. The grey pencil skirt she was wearing accentuated her round ass as her torso rested against her desk. I made no attempt to hold her down as I reached to undo my belt, and she, surprisingly, made no effort to move.

"Sabrina," I said, "I think you've needed someone to put you in your place for a long time, it might as well be me." And I brought my belt down on her still clothed ass.

It wasn't the first time I'd spanked a woman. A girlfriend in college loved it, but I was never truly disciplining her for bad behavior. This was different, my boss needed to learn a lesson.

When the belt smacked against her ass, Sabrina didn't cry out in anger so much as moan a "fuck you, you son of a bitch." I looked at her bent across the desk and her eyes were fixed on me through her glasses. I brought down the belt again, harder this time. She sucked in air through her teeth and then glared at me through the sensation.

"I'm not sure this belt is getting through to you, Sabrina," I said calmly. "Stand up and remove your skirt so I can give you a proper lesson."

She stood in front me, lowered her eyes and bit her lip. She undid the button on her skirt and the zipper. sliding it down her lean, bare legs past her heels, she stepped out of it. Under her skirt was a red lace thong.

"Remove everything, Sabrina," I continued, taking in the site of her half naked body. "Blouse, bra, and thong too."

"Fuck you," she said, but immediately began unbuttoning her shirt, chin to her chest, she watched me closely over the top of her glasses as her fingers worked the buttons. When she slid it off, stood there in just her bra, panties and high heels, I had to swallow hard, but I was determined to keep my role as dominant.
I gave her a steely glance. "Everything."

She hesitated and then reached behind her back undoing her bra. Her breasts were gorgeous, soft milk- white globes about the perfect size for my hands, with pink, erect nipples just waiting to be tweaked and twisted.

I kept myself from reaching out too eagerly, allowing her to finish her task. She slid her thong down her legs and revealed that she kept herself all but hairless, a thin strip of fine dark hair atop her now exposed cunt.

She went to remove her 4 inch heels, but I stopped her. "No," I said, "those stay on." She immediately stopped what she was doing and waited for a word from me.

Standing there, arms at her sides, head slightly bowed. Wearing nothing but her glasses and her heels, accentuated with what I now saw as the sluttiest shade of red lipstick and fingernail polish, and an almost out of place string of pearls around her neck, giving her an air of dignity at odds with her present position.
I took her by her delicate shoulders and pushed her down over her desk. She caught herself and rested her upper body on her forearms, her naked ass presented high in the air, aided by her heels.

I stepped behind her, put my foot between hers and pushed her legs apart. For the first time I could see how wet she was and I couldn't help but touch her. I pressed my palm against her sex and ground its flat surface against her cunt, feeling my hand slicken with her ample juices.

Sabrina moaned and gyrated her hips. This made me chuckle slightly as I watched her wanton transformation to bitch in heat from just plain bitch. "Jesus Sabrina, you're quite the submissive slut under all that show of authority, aren't you?"

She simply moaned in reply, which inspired me to remove my hand from her cunt and leave her wantonly pushing back against emptiness. I brought the belt down hard on the now bare flesh of her ass.

"Answer me, slut."

She whined from the dual stings of pain and humiliation. "I..." she hesitated, "I... don't know."

I brought the belt down hard again and the sharp sound of smacked flesh sounded in the air, followed shortly by her cry.

"Yu don't know if you're a submissive slut?" I taunted. "You certainly look like a submissive slut from where I'm standing."

Two more quick slaps with the leather from my belt and she fell forward on the desk, her arms giving way and her cheek pressed flat against the top. She reached one hand behind her, whether in an effort to shield her ass or soothe it, I didn't know, but I wasn't having any of it.

"Oh no, slut," I said. "Your ass is to remain exposed to me as long as I want it to be, and you will take whatever punishment I say you deserve for abusing your employees."

"No," she whimpered, "no, I'll be good." Her eyes were shut and completely unprompted she whispered, "I'll be your good girl."
"You're right, you will be." I grabbed her slender wrist and pulled it away from her reddening ass. Walking to the front of the desk, I removed my silk tie, held her wrists together in one of my hands and wrapped the tie around them, binding her wrists together above her head. She offered little resistance, as I finished the knot. It seemed that part of her wanted to stop this, but some other part, some deeper part wanted, or needed me to continue.

With her hands bound I was free to return working over the soft flesh of her ass which I did, repeatedly bringing my belt down as a stern punishment for her poor management of me and my colleagues.

Reddening the white skin as her howls filled the air. I could see the marks from the strap of my belt crisscross her delicate flesh.

I paused, panting, as she lay writhing across the desk, moaning almost inconsolably.

"Please..." she whimpered, "Please, I'm so close..."

I was dumb struck by her comment, but I noticed for the first times her thighs were damp with the overflow of her cunt. Intrigued as if I could get her to orgasm with the belt I smacked her again, harder this time and she shook violently as she cried out into the room. Again, the belt came down, this time focused to graze her pussy lips which she increasingly exposed and presented to my discipline.

This was enough to send her over as her body violently began to shake and she called out amid the non verbal shrieks, "Oh my god... that's it... oh god you bastard... I'm going to..." At that point I smacked her as hard as I had, and she finished her sentence by screaming

"Cuuuuuuummmmmm."

I watched in awe as my submissive slut of a boss melted into a pool of pleasure and pain as her body shook violently into orgasm from the mere fact of a spanking. Her face was agony and ecstasy, tears smeared the mascara from her closed eyes while her ruby red lips hung open gasping for air and crying out her divine anguish.

I sat back in her chair, leaving her splayed in front of me a heaving pile of broken and satisfied flesh. My cock was hard, of course, at the display, but fucking her exposed cunt seemed almost anticlimactic compared to the show I had just witnessed inspired by a whipping.

I stared at her body. From my angle I could see her spread legs leading up to her red ass and still quivering cunt. But I could also see her torso across the desk. Her breast smashed against the cold wood and her face with tear stained cheeks and panting mouth.

I stepped behind her and unzipped my pants, releasing my already hard cock. I kicked her legs apart, opening her wet pussy, took my cock in my hand and ran the

head up and down her exposed slit.

"You're good at telling people what to do, Sabrina," I mocked, "So why don't you tell me to fuck you."

She whimpered but otherwise remained silent. I brought the belt, still in my hand, down hard on her ass. Her legs quaked and a cry filled the room.

"You're not being a very good boss, Sabrina," I said, "You have a willing employee, but you're not making full use of his talents."

She mumbled something I couldn't hear, her whisper a combination of desire and exhaustion. I smacked her with the belt again. "Speak up, slut."

Tears filled her eyes, her face strained to get through the sting, but I could feel her cunt lips quiver and moisten. Dutifully she said, "Please fuck me."

I continued to wet the head of my cock just inside the lips of her cunt. "You can do better than that." I said, and I smacked her ass again.

"Fuck, fuck, fuck," she babbled, "please, fuck me, take me cunt, please just shove it inside me, I'll be a good girl."

With that I pressed into her, shoving my already aching cock into the tight folds of her wet flesh. She was tighter than expected, whether by nature or abstinence, I couldn't say, but she reacted as though she had been branded, lifting her head and arching her back, almost howling as I drove myself home. Pressed deep inside her, every inch of my thick cock was gripped by her flesh. I held myself there, wanting to revel in the feeling of it. I couldn't resist the idea of leaning forward and taking a firm hold of her hair, which had fallen out of its tie. Wrapping my hand in it I pulled back, making her arch her back even more. Holding her hair like a bridle with one hand, I brought the belt down on her ass with the other, as though I was a jockey whipping his mount.

She cried out again and I felt her inner muscles contract around my cock. The feeling was so divine I whipped her again, keeping firm hold of her hair. Her cries filled the room. Only then did I begin to fuck her in earnest, sliding out and pressing hard back into her, each thrust slow and deliberate and deep.

Occasionally I would bring the belt down again and she would sing out in that wonderful mix of pleasure and pain that would accompany a tension in her body that milked my ever invading cock.

Her vocals, became and incoherent mixture of pleas and commands. "Fuck me, yes, harder, harder, please, whatever you want, hurts so good, hurt me, fuck me, use me."
My own timing was getting better. And finally I brought the belt down hard on her backside, causing her to tighten just before I pressed into her, making my thrust rougher and more invasive. And this treatment proved to be all she needed as her body spasmed and collapsed into another orgasm as she all but screamed, "Fuuucckkkk Hurts so good!!"

I was pressing myself to the limit, but I had plans for this abusive slut. As she still shuddered from her orgasm, I pulled out, leaving her cunt obscenely fucking back against thin air. I pulled her by her hair to her feet, spun her toward me and then pushed her down to her knees.

Still holding her hair, she was panting with unfocused eyes as she looked up at me. Her makeup had smeared and her mouth hung open, and I took the opportunity to push my cock into it. Her eyes shot wide at first, but then closed as she sucked my cock as though it were a pacifier.

Her ordeal had left her exhausted, so it was up to me to control the action. I used both hands to hold her head as I proceeded to fuck her mouth. Her moans vibrated through me as I could feel my cock swell against her tongue.

Finally I pulled out, letting my cock erupt onto her face. The first spurt splashed across her nose and glasses, the second more directly on her lips. I shoved back into her mouth for the remaining amount. Whether happy to be used or just oblivious, she sucked and swallowed the rest.

I fell back into her desk chair as I released her, my own legs giving out. She fell back on her haunches, resting against the drawers of her oak desk. Cum covered her face and dripped down to her breasts. She looked past me with a vacant, satisfied expression.

I reached forward and ran a finger over a glob of cum

on her cheek and shoved it into her mouth. Without thinking, she sucked my finger clean.

"Good girl, Sabrina," I said as I fed her my cum from my finger, "Now get to work rewriting that copy. I'm going home."

ISLAND OF SUBMISSION
Submission Bdsm Story

Safely hidden -- or so she imagined -- behind the gardener's shed in a quiet corner of the school grounds Kerry leisurely exhales the smoke from a surreptitious cigarette. Final exams finished there's no harm in kicking back and relaxing. She's taken great pains to avoid detection, doesn't want to blot her academic record and jeopardise a promised university place.

An unexpected hand on her shoulder makes Kerry yelp in fright, turning quickly to discover who has tracked her down. Could be worse, is Kerry's first thought. Rather than a teacher, Kieran, the rather dishy assistant groundsman looms over her. Kerry is far from the only female sixth former to appreciate his saturnine good looks.

"You scared me," gasps Kerry, hurriedly grinding the incriminating evidence under foot.

"Bit pointless," observes Kieran, "you've been caught young lady. We'd better go inside and have a little chat."

Kerry feels a stab of anxiety; he surely isn't intending to report this transgression? With considerable trepidation she follows the dark haired young man into the gloomy confines of his workplace.

"You're not going to..." Kerry lets the sentence hang unfinished, doing her best to project an impression of wide-eyed innocence.

"Tell on you to the teachers, should do by rights," responds Kieran laconically.

"I'm 18, legally old enough to smoke," ventures Kerry with hint of defiance.

"Old enough for a lot of things, but still against school rules. You should know being one of the clever ones in the top set."

"How could you possibly be aware of that?" Kerry is shocked.

"By listening, working on the flowerbeds outside the classroom windows I hear all sorts -- quite enough to know how much trouble you could be in."

"So you'll let me off," whispers Kerry beguiling.

"Never said so," replies Kieran brusquely. "I might choose not to inform the headteacher, but you still deserve to be punished -- smoking's a filthy habit, it's not as if your generation aren't educated about the dangers."

"You're right," Kerry looks downcast, "but what do you mean, punished?"

"Properly, physically, not just for what you've done, as a future deterrent."

"What, like spank me or something? You can't be serious, no one does that anymore."

"Don't seem like you've much of a choice," says Kieran coolly -- think of the consequences if you don't agree."

Kerry does, shuddering at the prospect of her parent's reaction -- "not angry, just very disappointed," followed by weeks of passive aggressive guilt tripping. She can't stand it, better to get this over with.

"Alright", she agrees cautiously, "but you promise not

to ever let on?"

"I'll keep my word so long as you do what you're told," he answers firmly, "start by bending over that workbench."

Hesitantly Kerry leans forward, staring fixedly ahead, weight supported on her forearms. Glossy, shoulder-length fair hair partly obscuring her pretty face, uniform blouse tight against straining breasts, skirt - far shorter than regulation length - revealing taught thighs and long straight legs; an altogether enticing prospect.

"Like this?" she enquires timidly.

"Perfect," replies Kieran rolling up his sleeves to reveal tanned forearms, "now get that skirt up girl."

"No, you mustn't make me..."

"You agreed to comply," his tone is so compelling the reluctant girl's fingers scramble to obey, revealing an absolute peach of a bottom covered by dark tights and tiny white knickers.

Kieran experiences an immediate stiffening of his manhood and momentarily can't trust himself to speak, instead placing a restraining hand on of Kerry's slender waist he brings the other sharply down across those deliciously pert nether cheeks.

"OOF!" Kerry grits her teeth, scared to cry out lest someone hear and investigate. Further spanks follow, his work-calloused palm rhythmically slapping her buttocks. Kerry's feet stamp in mute protest as her poor bottom begins to smart and sting.

He stops. She gives an audible sigh. Is that it? Wasn't too bad, bum's smarting yet Kerry is also aware of a rather more enjoyable sensation burgeoning between her thighs.

"That was just the warm-up," asserts Kieran, "we'll have these down," he tugs at the tights and knickers, "and you'll take the rest on the bare."

"The rest! I thought..."

"Don't care what you thought. Time I've finished that bottom's going to be so sore you'll never look at a cigarette again."

Kieran's hard hand applied to bare flesh takes the

hurt to a whole new level. Kerry struggles futilely as her delightful derriere burns hotter, yelping and protesting

-- no chance of her staying quiet now - at each subsequent slap.

Another interlude, Kerry looks reproachfully over her shoulder, eyes wet and arse glowing red. Confused by being simultaneously sore and sexually aroused, can he see how wet she is?

Of course Kieran can, and plans to do something about it, just soon as he's concluded Kerry's chastisement in the traditional manner.

"Six of the best should finish you off nicely," he states, ominously swishing a thin, whippy cane through the air. "Pulled these from the rose beds, not really long enough but needs must." Kerry groans in dismay, no point in pleading, she's little choice but to submit.

"Hold the edge of the bench and push your bottom up," he commands.

She obeys but Kieran's not yet satisfied. "Higher," he says sharply. Screwing her eyes tight shut to avoid seeing the scary bamboo Kerry goes up onto her toes and somehow manages to force her posterior further into the air.

It takes all of the young man's self restraint not to fuck her there and then. Instead Kieran delivers the promised half dozen cane cuts to her already well-smacked bottom. Mild in comparison with some he's applied to willing spankees in the past, Kerry is – for now -- a novice and this caning primarily to ensure her complete compliance with what will follow...

"Done and dusted," he observes as the cane clatters to the floor. Strong hands grasp her hips and Kieran stoops to kiss each brightly burning orb. "You done good girl, turned you on didn't it?'

Blushing in excitement and humiliation Kerry is lost for words. Right then her blouse buttons pop open, giving up the struggle to contain her boobs His hands move to free them from her bra, deliciously teasing hard nipples. Face flushed with pent-up desire, Kerry makes no protest,

"Reckon you need a thorough seeing to young lady," says Kieran loosening his belt. Kerry risks another glimpse over her shoulder just in time to see an impressively erect cock spring from his jeans. Christ, she'll never to be able to fit all that in! Kieran's fingers slide between her juice-slicked labia, thumb circling her pulsing clit.

"Reckon you can take this?" queries Kieran, correctly interpreting her thoughts; a condom wrapper flutters to the ground.

"I'll try," Kerry nervously pushes her hot little tush back towards her erstwhile tormentor, "I'm not a virgin," she adds quickly. Up to a point, her besotted boyfriend usually fumbles the foreplay then comes far too quickly, leaving Kerry frustrated and forced to compete the job herself.

"Good girl," grunts the groundsman, easing the tip of his cock into her velvety slot.

"OMG!" she exclaims in delight as he slowly slides it in, gently stretching her deliciously tight pussy until she's accommodated the full length and girth. He pauses to let Kelly adjust to it filling her sex, lividly marked arse pressing hard against his washboard abdomen. Begins to thrust unhurriedly back and forth, squeezing her tits, carefully upping the pace. Oh my, the sensation is incredible, like nothing Kerry has felt before. Better even than when fingering herself while indulging a favourite submissive fantasy - the reality of which far exceeds her dreams.

"You're a bad girl," gasps Kieran, in thrall to desire and screwing her faster now, clasping her tenderised bottom cheeks and unleashing a surge of sexual sensation within Kerry's trembling body. Is she a bad girl? Kerry wonders distractedly, if this is what happens to them she'd like to be.

"Oh yes," she yells exultantly. Kieran feels her entire body spasm, his cock gripped clenched tight in her pulsating pussy as Kerry reaches a crescendo and convulsively comes.

Both breathing heavily they take a moment to recover then, with him still rock hard inside, the young woman lasciviously wriggles her hips. Brimming with lust and the vigour of youth Kelly's already good to go again. It's Kieran's turn to feel his arousal surge out of control, pushing hard and deep into her lithe body his own climax fast approaching.

"Oh God yes, go on you bastard, fuck my pussy," screams Kerry, astonished at her industrial language and loss of control. She feels his prick pump inside her, dimly hears an animal growl of satisfaction; his or hers, it doesn't matter. Another shuddering orgasm, Kerry's education is complete.

"Wow, our best role-play yet," Kerry says a few minutes later, attempting to straighten her clothes in the cramped space of their garden shed, "goodness, I can hardly stand up."

"Lucky you kept your old school uniform and it still fits," replies her husband appreciatively.

"Only just, my bust seems to have grown bigger over the last decade."

"What scene shall we try next?"

"Something more comfortable," pleads Kelly, "I'm not really into unforgiving work surfaces and dust, I want a little luxury for a change."

"Hmm, perhaps a serving girl spanked over her master's four-poster bed -- we could book a night in one of those fancy boutique hotels?"

"Oh, yes please -- I think I've still got my old waitress outfit from when I worked in that tea room during the

Uni hols. Little white apron and cap, bit like a maid..."

"Sounds good, I could go down on you, seduce the servant."

"Or I you, service the master, they're not mutually exclusive and I'm getting spanked whatever aren't I?"

"Without a shadow of a doubt."

GOLDEN ASSIGNMENT
Mdom Bdsm Story

"The key is anticipation," Mistress Andrea said, preening her long, strawberry-blonde hair slightly and glorying in the astonished gazes of her fellow dommes. She held their gaze with her own green eyes, reveling in their awe. "That was what really took the longest, training Robyn to not just obey me instinctively, but to anticipate my desires before I even expressed them. Needless to say, it wasn't easy."

Robyn walked over to her, totally naked, holding a goblet. She had absolutely no hair at all, either on her head or body; Andrea liked her pets smooth and clean. "Mistress wants more wine," she said dully, her blue eyes vacant. She was totally in subspace now, Andrea knew, absolutely incapable of understanding anything but obedience.

"Thank you, Robyn," Andrea said, taking the goblet of wine. "See, this is what I'm talking about," Andrea said, sipping at the drink. "I didn't even need to inform her that I was thirsty; she simply picked up on subconscious cues in my body language and went to go get me something refreshing. It's all about anticipation."

Joan took a long moment to find her voice. "And she doesn't..." She kept staring at robyn as the slavegirl walked off behind Andrea to handle her duties, seeming absolutely bowled over with the sheer audacity of Andrea's achievements. No surprise, really. Joan was always a bit of a 'soft' domme, far too lenient on her pets. She certainly couldn't have imagined the kind of training regimen that Andrea had put robyn through. "She doesn't notice anything unusual? Anything at all?"

Andrea laughed. "She's not capable of noticing anything at all, Joan. I told you, the amount of hypnosis she's been through, she probably doesn't even know the rest of you exist. I'm the absolute center of Robyn's world." Andrea didn't even bother looking at robyn as she spoke. She was confident that Robyn was handling her slave duties, there was no need to oversee her personally. In fact, that was the point of this whole endeavor. "Of course, it's not just hypnosis. There's more to it than that, but--"

Robyn came up alongside Andrea, breaking into her conversation. "Mistress wants another piece of cheese," she said dully. She held out a plate, and Andrea gratefully popped a bit of cheddar into her mouth.

"Thank you, Robyn," she said. "Where was I? Oh, of course. The training regimen. It's not just hypnosis. It's a combination of hypnosis and sensory overload. We all know that 'subspace' is the point where a submissive loses the ability to resist completely. I'm just making use of that state to facilitate her hypnotic conditioning. The two work together in a kind of synergy, putting the submissive into a whole new level of obedience--one where her core identity can be totally reshaped. Triggers and post-hypnotic suggestions are only the beginning. I can reshape someone's entire personality, if I want."

"Is...is that true?" Kara said, looking over at Robyn's naked body. Robyn nodded her head absently, understanding that the question was directed at her even through the haze of trance. Andrea practically glowed with pride; certainly, she was proud of her own ability to bring Robyn to this state, but she was equally proud of Robyn's talents as a slave. She couldn't have taken just anyone and turned them into the perfect pet. No, Andrea needed to find a diamond in the rough, and while she might have turned out flawless work, Robyn was the diamond she found.

"Unbelievable," Kara said. "I never would have imagined it possible if I hadn't seen it with my own eyes, but this is the proof." Andrea was a little surprised at just how astonished Kara seemed. She'd seen Kara with her pet, Dana, and while nobody was as obedient as Robyn, Dana did a pretty good job of coming close. "Tell us..." Kara's eyes flicked back and forth between Robyn and Andrea. "Tell us more about how you did it."

Robyn said, "Mistress wants a backrub," as she set the cheese tray down. Andrea shifted position on the couch to allow Robyn room to slide in behind her, and robyn's talented fingers were soon working on her shoulders.

"Mmmm, that's nice, pet," Andrea said. "I started with hypnosis, of course. I put her under with a long induction, longer than usual." She sighed softly at the way Robyn's hands relaxed her muscles. "I wanted her to be very deep for me by the time we started playing. Once I was satisfied that she was at the right level of trance, I tied her up."

"Couldn't you have just used a freeze trigger?" Joan asked. Joan was big into mind-play, less so into the physical aspects of BDSM. She barely even spanked her pets.

"I wanted to...mmm..." Robyn worked the muscles of Andrea's lower back in just the way she liked. "I wanted to accentuate the feeling of helplessness. She needed to be physically as well as mentally controlled." Which was why Joan would never have a hope in hell of making her pet, mia, this obedient. "Then I started the sensory stimulation. Clothespins on the breasts, a vibrating butt plug up her ass...I used the crop on her for a long while. All the while, whispering suggestions. She was trembling like a leaf, weren't you, Robyn?"

"Yes, Mistress," Robyn said. "Mistress remembers me sinking into deep, helpless hypnotic trance. Mistress remembers turning me into an obedient slavegirl. Mistress remembers brainwashing me into a perfect slut."

Andrea sighed happily at the memory of the day when Robyn's will broke completely, when even the subconscious resistance melted away and she became the perfect slave. "I kept alternating like that, physical stimulation and mental stimulation. It took the better part of a day, but by the end of it, Robyn didn't even know how to come out of trance anymore. After that, it was all just a matter of training."

"And she doesn't notice the trigger at all?" Joan asked.

"Not consciously, no. She just obeys." Andrea rolled her eyes just a little at that. Surely Joan knew how post-hypnotic triggers worked by now? Anyway, it wasn't like she used many on robyn. She didn't need to. Robyn anticipated her every desire now.

"Mistress wants her shirt off," Robyn said. Andrea lifted her arms as Robyn pulled it up over her shoulders and off. Robyn returned to her rubbing, now able to press her hands directly against Andrea's flesh. "Mistress wants her bra off as well," Robyn said, unsnapping the hook and sliding the brassiere off.

"This is just...just incredible," Kara said, leaning forward in her chair. "Is there anything she won't do? Any suggestion she wouldn't be able to integrate with the new personality?"

"None at all," Andrea said, smiling softly as she felt Robyn's hands reach around to touch her breasts. "Everything just seems perfectly natural to her. On a subconscious level, she knows she needs to obey the commands, and her conscious mind will construct any rationalization necessary to make her think it's all her own idea." That wasn't exactly how it worked, of course; Andrea knew for a fact that Robyn didn't have any conscious mind left to rationalize with. But she just needed to explain it all in a way that Kara would understand, so she used the jargon of 'rationalizing' to describe it. It was all perfectly simple.

"Mistress wants her breasts sucked," Robyn said, and Andrea shifted herself around to face her pet. She leaned back, letting Robyn lick at her nipples with her oh-so-talented tongue.

"This is the best part," she said, feeling Robyn's soft, kitten licks and occasional nips. "She knows so...ohhh...so perfectly what pleases me. Her mind...well, what's left of her mind, it's..." Andrea gasped just a little as she felt Robyn's tongue tracing around her aureola. "It's working overtime to anticipate my needs."

"Mistress wants to be naked now," Robyn said, and Andrea knew from the ache in her pussy that her slave had predicted her needs perfectly yet again. Andrea didn't even wait for Robyn's help, she just unfastened her buttons and kicked her pants off urgently. Her panties □uickly followed. Joan and Kara were probably a little surprised by the show, but it wasn't like they hadn't seen anything like it before. It was perfectly fine to get naked in front of the other two women. (Robyn, of course, didn't count.)

"But...but..." Joan seemed to be trying to put something very difficult into words. "But why would you do it?"
Of course. That was Joan, the big softy. Always trying to make her pets whimper with pleasure, stroking and pampering them like housecats. She didn't understand what it was like to be a real domme, truly in charge of every thought in her slave's head. "Mistress wants to bend over the couch now so i can finger-fuck her," Robyn said.

"I'd have thought it was obvious, Joan," Andrea said as she shifted position. "I want to control her, completely and...ohhhh..." She spread her legs a little wider to allow Robyn's fingers better access to her cunt. "Completely and, nnnh...totally, want to, oh yes that's good, want to have a sex slave who really..." Her pussy was slick and juicy now, soaking Robyn's fingers as they slid in and out. Andrea couldn't help herself, she just kept thrusting at Robyn's hand. The other dommes would understand, they wouldn't mind that she was presenting her hungry, aching cunt to them and pressing her face into the cushions of the sofa. They'd understand it was all part of her demonstration, all just another way of showing just how much control she had over Robyn. "...who really knows the true meaning of obedience."

"But don't you want to give her orders?" Kara asked. "I mean, to other people, it doesn't look like you're in charge. I always thought showing off your dominance was half the fun."

Andrea let out a loud, animalistic moan into the fabric of the couch as Robyn began circling her clit with her other hand. "I am showing off my dominance. That's the, oh fuck YES, oh..." She momentarily lost her train of thought in a burst of hot, red pleasure. "That's the point. I'm so in charge I don't need to give orders."

"Mistress wants her ass whipped," Robyn said, taking her finger off of Andrea's clit and reaching over to the table for the new riding crop that Kara had brought to show them. She picked it up, swished it in the air experimentally, and then brought it down on Andrea's ass hard. Andrea moaned, her pussy clenching around Robyn's still-thrusting fingers.

"I didn't just...oh...didn't just want to give her orders," Andrea said, her voice unsteady as the pleasure built towards a crescendo. "I wanted total control. Complete power." The crop came down again...and again...and again, each snapping blow reddening her flesh as it mingled with the mounting orgasm. "And I have that with Robyn, now." She closed her eyes, loving the sensation of being naked, bent over the couch and finger-fucked while Robyn whipped her ass. "I'm in charge of everything," she said, and the realization of just how true that was sent her over the edge into orgasm.

It felt like an eternity before she finally came back from the heights of pleasure, her legs rubbery as she continued to bend over the couch. She couldn't see the expression on the other two dommes' faces, but she knew they had to be impressed by the degree of control she'd demonstrated over her pet.

"I have to admit," Kara said, "I'm amazed." Andrea felt like she was glowing with pride. She could hear the quiet awe in Kara's voice, and more than a little arousal, too. "This is certainly every bit as impressive as you told us it'd be, Robyn." Andrea almost laughed. Kara was so worked up by their little display that she'd even gotten the names mixed up.

Joan said, "Ditto for me. But, um, watching you two at work has left me wanting to try her out for myself." She let out a little giggle. "Any chance I could borrow her for a few minutes, just to let loose a little tension?"

Andrea beamed with pride. They understood, then. They understood just how special a piece of conditioning this was, how much time and effort had gone into it all. They understood what a powerful, what a commanding hypnodomme she was. She opened her mouth, but Robyn had already anticipated her needs before she could speak. "Mistress wants to lick Joan's pussy," Robyn said, and Andrea turned and crawled, naked, towards Joan's waiting body. Robyn always knew what Andrea needed. That was what made her such a good slave, Andrea thought as she knelt in front of Joan and begin to softly lick. Part of her almost wished that Robyn could be consciously aware of her complete submission, but Andrea knew, deep down, that it was so much hotter that she didn't realize how enslaved she was.

"Mistress wants the strap-on inside her," Robyn said dully, and Mistress Andrea presented her cunt to be fucked.

9 798565 456486